FRANKIE'S MAGIC FOOTBALL

FRANKIE'S MAGIC FOOTBALL

OLYMPIC FLAME CHASE

FRANK LAMPARD

LITTLE, BROWN BOOKS FOR YOUNG READERS
www.lbkids.co.uk

LITTLE, BROWN BOOKS FOR YOUNG READERS

First published in Great Britain in 2016 by Hodder and Stoughton

1 3 5 7 9 10 8 6 4 2

A CIP catalogue record for this book
is available from the British Library.

ISBN 978-1-51020-110-1

Typeset in Cantarell by M Rules
Printed and bound in Great Britain by
Clays Ltd, St Ives plc

The paper and board used in this book are made
from wood from responsible sources.

Little, Brown Books for Young Readers
An imprint of
Hachette Children's Group
Part of Hodder and Stoughton
Carmelite House
50 Victoria Embankment
London EC4Y 0DZ

An Hachette UK Company
www.hachette.co.uk

www.hachettechildrens.co.uk

To my mum Pat, who encouraged me
to do my homework in between kicking
a ball all around the house, and is still
with me every step of the way.

*Welcome to a fantastic
Fantasy League – the greatest
football competition ever held
in this world or any other!*

*You'll need four on a team,
so choose carefully. This is a lot
more serious than a game in the
park. You'll never know who your
next opponents will be, or
where you'll face them.*

*So lace up your boots, players,
and good luck! The whistle's
about to blow!*

The Ref

PART ONE

CHAPTER 1

"Wow, Frankie," his mum gasped. "This place looks amazing!"

The school hall was packed with other families. Frankie spotted his teacher, Mr Donald, beaming with pride.

The hall did look great. The whole school had made decorations themed around the Olympic Games. Five interlocking coloured hoops hung from the ceiling in the shape of the Olympic rings. A spinning globe showed all the different cities where the competition had taken place. There was even a special display about the latest Games.

"Did you know," said Louise, "the first modern Olympics were held in Athens, Greece, in 1896?"

"I didn't," said her father, smiling.

"But the Games are much older than that," Louise continued. "They began in ancient Greece, in the eighth century BC."

"Fascinating," said Frankie's brother, rolling his eyes. "I can't believe I have to come to school on a Saturday!"

Frankie's dad put an arm around Kevin's shoulders. "Don't you want to watch your brother in the sports day?"

Kevin glowered. "I can think of a million things I'd rather be doing." He began to count on his fingers. "Washing dishes, weeding the garden, cutting my toenails, cutting *the dog's* toenails ..."

Max yipped near Frankie's ankles. "Don't worry, boy," said Frankie. "We won't let him near your claws."

"Can I go outside?" said Kevin. "It's really hot in here."

"Just you stay out of trouble," said Frankie's mum.

Kevin smirked and ran off.

He doesn't know how *to stay out of trouble,* thought Frankie. He caught sight of Charlie and his family coming towards him, their cheeks pink with the heat. Charlie wafted his face with one of his hands.

"You'd be cooler if you took off your gloves, Charles," said his dad.

"But would I be ready to stop a football?" said Charlie.

"Suit yourself," replied his dad. "Though I'm not sure you're allowed to wear them for the shot-put."

Charlie frowned. "I hadn't thought of that ..."

As part of their Olympics term, everyone had been trying out new sports. At first Frankie hadn't been too keen — playing other sports meant *not* playing football — but he'd really enjoyed the running and the high jump. Today all the training would be put to the test in the sports day. Five schools from across town were competing, and there was going to be a medal ceremony at the end, just like in the real Olympics. Charlie's event was the shot-put. Louise was doing long jump, and Frankie would be taking part in a football obstacle course — a test of sprinting, dribbling, heading and shooting. He couldn't wait!

As they left the hall through the double doors at the back, Frankie saw the school's Olympic torch burning on its stand in the playground. Mr Donald had told them that the real torch was lit every four years in a place called Olympia in Greece. Runners then carried it in a relay to whichever country was hosting the Games. Sometimes they ran thousands of miles! The torch never went out and symbolized the spirit of the Games.

Mr Donald clapped his hands. "Right, parents, please take your places on the sports pitch. Kids — go and get ready. The games will begin in twenty minutes!"

Frankie and his friends warmed up round the side of the school in the shade. They used his magic football, passing it between them, dribbling it around, and heading it back and forth.

"Are you sure it's safe to have your football in school?" said Charlie, stretching to catch it. "You know what it can do." The ball had taken them on adventures all around the world – Australia, Brazil and even Lapland.

"I didn't want to leave it at home in case Kevin got his hands on it," said Frankie.

"Good thinking," said Louise. "But the last thing we need today is a magical adventure."

"As long as we're careful, it should be—"

Something hit him on the shoulder and Frankie cried out.

His arm was soaked, and on the ground he saw a blue scrap of rubber.

"Is that a water balloon?" he said.

A red one shot past and

splatted into the wall near Charlie's head.

"Who's throwing them?" said Louise.

Frankie heard a chuckle and he knew at once who it belonged to. Kevin appeared on the flat school roof with his friends Rob and Matt. They each had a carrier bag filled with bulging water balloons.

"You shouldn't be up there," called Louise.

"Don't get your knickers in a twist," said Kevin. "We found the caretaker's ladder. We're just having a bit of fun."

"Gonna cool everyone down a bit," added Rob.

"Ready to get soaked?" asked Matt. All three took out a water balloon.

"Run!" said Charlie.

Frankie scooped up his football and they darted out of the way as the bombs rained down. Frankie felt the water splash his legs, and saw Charlie try to bat one out of the air with his hand. It exploded over his head, completely drenching him.

"Not funny!" Charlie yelled.

As they crossed the playground, Frankie heard footsteps pounding after them. *They must have climbed down!* Frankie could see the crowds of parents and competitors gathered ahead. Even Kevin wouldn't dare be seen by Mr Donald. He looked back – his brother was puffing hard.

Something snagged at Frankie's foot and he tripped headlong on to the grass. The ball fell from his hands as he rolled across the ground. Picking himself up again, he saw Kevin draw back his fist, gripping another water bomb.

"Nowhere to run, Frankenstein," said Kevin.

He chucked the balloon, and Frankie ducked. It shot right over

his head, and Frankie heard a
fizzling sound. He looked over his
shoulder and saw that the school's
Olympic torch was smoking, the
remains of the water balloon
hanging off the end.

"You've really done it this time,"
said Charlie.

"See ya!" said Rob, backing off from Kevin's side.

"Nice one, mate," chuckled Matt. He turned and ran away. So much for being Kevin's friends.

Frankie's brother stood frozen to the spot, his face drained of blood. Frankie wasn't surprised.

Mr Donald was striding towards them, looking very angry indeed.

CHAPTER 2

"What's going on here?" shouted their teacher.

Kevin blushed. He tried to hide the rest of his water balloons behind his back, but it was too late.

"Sorry, sir – I was just ..."

He trailed off as the sky darkened overhead. Frankie felt a shiver across his bare skin, and a gusting wind kicked up across the school field. He glanced up and saw black clouds rolling in front of the sun.

"That's weird ..." he mumbled.

A sudden crack of thunder made everyone cry out, and then the heavens opened. Rain lashed down and people ran from the edge of the school field to scramble for shelter. Some went to the sports pavilion, others headed for the main school buildings. Frankie saw his parents trying to shield themselves with their event programmes. No one had even thought to bring an umbrella because it was such a lovely day.

Max scampered across the field to where Frankie was.

"I'll deal with you later," said Mr Donald, pointing to Kevin. "Get inside with everyone else."

Lightning flashed across the sky, followed by another deep rumble of thunder. The world had turned grey. Puddles were already forming across the ground, and water poured from the gutters. Charlie and Louise joined Frankie. They hurried back towards the school doors as more lightning forked down.

A rush of wet bodies pressed into the school entrance. Max

shook himself, splashing everyone with water droplets.

"I don't like this," muttered Louise. "It started right after the torch went out. Almost like ... magic."

"Just a coincidence," said Charlie. "The football was nowhere near, was it?"

Frankie swallowed. Where *was* the football?

"Uh-oh," he said, edging back to the door. He'd dropped it when he was running from Kevin. He scanned the playground, but couldn't see anything through the downpour.

"Quiet down, please," said Mr Donald. Gradually the chatter stopped. "I'm sorry to say the weather is against us. We'll have to cancel our sports day."

A sigh rose from the crowd. Louise and Charlie looked worried.

"They can't," said Frankie. "Everyone's been getting ready for weeks!"

"Let's head to the main hall," said Mr Donald. "We'll get everyone a hot drink."

Groaning, the parents and kids began to file along the corridor. Frankie hung back. Louise was right. This weather wasn't natural. Just a couple of minutes ago the sun had been shining in a bright blue sky.

"I have to go back outside for the football," he said.

"Out there?" said Charlie, shaking his head. "It's not safe."

Lightning flashed through the clouds. Frankie had never seen anything like it. "If the magic football caused this, it's up to me to fix it," he said.

"I'm coming with you," said Louise.

Charlie lifted his gloves in front of his face. "Even *these* can't save us from lightning, but I'm not letting you two go alone."

Frankie pushed open the door and ran out into the swirling rain. He was soaked to the skin in seconds. He looked around for the ball.

Where is it?

"There!" pointed Louise.

The ball was resting underneath the football goal at the edge of the field.

Max bounded off after it.

"Come back, boy!" cried Frankie.

He thinks it's a game ...

But his little dog didn't listen. He was about ten metres away when the sky exploded with light. The flash was so bright that Frankie had

to cover his eyes with his arm. With his eyes tight shut, he heard a yelp. It could only have come from Max. *Oh no ...*

With dread rising in his chest, Frankie looked back out across the playground. A column of smoke rose up from the place where the football had been. The very spot where Frankie's dog had been heading.

"Max?" he cried, rushing forwards. Had the lightning hit him?

To his relief, Max came padding through the smoke, his fur standing on end. The football was smoking. Frankie stabbed at it with his toe. It rolled slowly towards the goalposts, coming to a stop beneath the top bar. As it did, there was a shimmer of light and the world on the other side vanished. Louise and Charlie let out a gasp. On the other side of the goalpost was a mass of swirling inky blackness – a doorway into the dark. Not what you expected to see on a summer's day!

Frankie looked nervously over his shoulder. Had anyone in the school noticed? Fortunately, he could see that they'd all crowded around a dinner lady carrying a tray of sandwiches. He glanced back at the portal. Where did it lead to? Frankie felt a tingle of excitement in his stomach. The football usually opened these entrances for a good reason.

Slowly, he walked towards the goalpost. "We need to get this sports day back on track," said Frankie. "And I bet the answer

lies on the other side of this goal. Ready for another adventure?"

"Always ready," said Charlie.

Louise clenched her jaw and nodded.

Together, they stepped into the darkness.

CHAPTER 3

The perfumed scent of incense was
the first thing Frankie noticed. In
the dim flicker of firelight, rows of
huge marble columns rose above
them to a roof spanned with thick
wooden beams. The air was cool
and dry. He wasn't wearing his PE
kit any more. Instead he had a plain
short tunic fastened with a clip at
the shoulder, and leather sandals.

The others were dressed the same way, though Charlie still wore his gloves.

"Where are we?" he said, and his voice echoed off the stone.

"I have no idea," whispered Charlie.

Max's claws clacked on the marble floor as he sniffed the base of a column.

Louise was peering at the columns closely. "I think this is a temple," she said. "This stonework reminds me of something I read about in History."

Side by side, they passed between the pillars into a gloomy,

30

wide-open space. Frankie drew a
sharp breath.

"Wow!" said Charlie.

At the other end of the aisle was
the biggest statue Frankie had ever
seen. It was a man on a throne. A
sculpted wreath of leaves sat on
his head. He clutched a staff with a
carved eagle at the top. His entire
body was painted dazzling gold,
and his eyes shone blue. His spare
hand was open, and on it rested
a smaller statue of a woman with
wings. She held a real, flaming
torch in her hand.

"The man is Zeus," said Louise.
"King of the Greek gods."

"We're in Greece?" said Frankie.

"Ancient Greece," said Louise. "It makes perfect sense."

"Does it?" said Max.

"Hello, boy," said Frankie. He always liked going on their adventures, because the magic allowed his dog to talk.

"Zeus was the god of thunder and lightning," Louise explained. "His temple was at Olympia, where the ancient Olympic Games were held. That woman on his hand is Nike."

"Like the trainers?" said Charlie.

Louise nodded. "She's the goddess of victory."

Frankie pointed at the torch in Nike's hand. "So that's a real Olympic flame," he said. "That must be why we're here. To get the flame and take it home."

"Isn't that stealing?" said Charlie, looking worried.

Frankie sighed. "I guess we could bring it back again afterwards."

"I don't think we have a choice," said Louise.

Max ran up to the bottom of the statue and craned his neck. "How are we going to get up there, anyway?"

Frankie peered around. They must have lit the torch somehow. "Perhaps there's a ladder."

Louise walked around to the back of the statue. "Here!" she called.

Frankie and the others joined her. The back of the statue was covered by a hanging drape, and there were wooden steps leading up to the place where the statue sat.

Max pricked his ears. "Did you hear something?"

Frankie shook his head and peered back into the temple. He couldn't see anyone.

"Let's be quick," he whispered, and began to climb the steps. They creaked softly under his feet. He reached the top and edged along the chair's seat. From up here, the statue seemed even larger.

Frankie clambered on to Zeus's leg, trying not to look down.

The torch flickered in the goddess's hand as Frankie reached out towards it.

Almost there . . .

Suddenly he heard a noise coming from his left — it sounded like the ruffle of wings. A shape emerged from behind a pillar. It was a boy — but he was flying!

Frankie jerked back and wheeled his arms, almost falling.

"Oh no, you don't!" said the stranger. As he shot past, he snatched the torch away. Frankie saw he was wearing sandals with tiny wings on the sides, and in his other hand he had what looked like a short staff or wand, engraved with snakes. "What do you think you're doing?"

"We were ... I was just ..."

"I should turn you in to the stewards!" said the boy. "Stealing from a temple will get you locked up."

"Who *are* you?" Charlie called up.

The boy frowned. "Don't you know?"

Charlie shook his head. The boy pointed to his winged sandals. "Aren't these a clue?"

"Ah!" said Louise. "You're Hermes! I remember you from our lesson. You're the god of mischief!"

"Correct!" said the boy. "Wind-footed Hermes. God of mischief, messengers, the wind. But mainly mischief." He grinned. "And that's

why I'm going to tell on you."
Hermes began to fly towards the
doors of the temple.

"Wait!" called Frankie. "Please
don't. There must be something we
can do. Our Olympic sports day has
been ruined. We need the torch to
make it right again."

Hermes scowled, flying even
higher. "Well, perhaps . . ."

"Anything," said Frankie.

Hermes grinned. "If you can win
an event here at *my* sports day,
then I won't tell. I might even let
you take the flame."

Frankie glanced down at the
others. Win at the real Olympic

Games? Charlie shrugged and Max wagged his tail. Louise nodded.

What choice do we have?

"We'll do it," said Frankie. "Let the games begin!"

CHAPTER 4

"I don't trust him," grumbled
Charlie, as Frankie jumped down
the remaining steps from the
statue. Hermes was hovering by the
temple doors.

"Me neither," said Frankie.

They ran between the columns to
the doors, painted with pictures of
gods and monsters.

"Wait a moment," said Hermes.

He pointed his wand at Louise, who flinched.

"What are you going to—"

The wand glowed and a stream of smoke shot from the end towards her. As it cleared, she was wearing a small round cap, her hair tucked underneath.

"Girls aren't allowed to compete in the events, but you'll probably pass for a boy now," said Hermes. "Right, I'll be watching you. Good luck!"

He shot back into the dark interior of the temple.

Frankie pushed open the doors and sucked in a breath as bright sunlight flooded over him. Outside were loads of other buildings and statues, painted in bright colours. People in togas streamed in the same direction, chattering excitedly.

"Are dogs allowed here?" asked Max.

Frankie heard the clip–clop of hooves and saw two chestnut horses being led along the street. No one batted an eyelid at his little dog.

"Just don't wee on any statues," he said.

The smells of hot oil and pastry mixed with smoke and incense. They walked past stalls stocked with jewellery and snacks and what looked like little pottery ornaments.

They hurried on, joining the crowds. "Try to keep a low profile," said Frankie as his dog trotted between feet.

"The Olympics were held here every four years," Louise said. "Athletes came from all over Greece to take part."

They passed beneath a stone archway, and on the other side the landscape opened up to reveal a huge athletics ground as big as a football stadium and covered in sand. Frankie's heart swelled. *What a place!* To think, they were back

where the Olympics all began —
fair play, sportsmanship, noble
competition . . .

Stone seats were cut into the
steep banks on three sides. There
were more torches lit in stands,
even though it was daytime.

"Those are for the judges," said
Louise, pointing to wooden towers
standing around the outside.

Charlie leant across to Frankie
and muttered behind his glove.

"Lucky *someone* was paying
attention in Donaldo's lessons."

As everyone took their seats,
a band struck up a tune. From a
hut several young men emerged,

walking proudly towards the sandy arena. They each held a discus in their right hand, and were being led by an old man carrying a wooden rod.

"The discus! That's my event!" said Charlie. He ran off and joined the back of the queue.

There were no seats left, so Frankie and Louise stood with other onlookers. He peered around at the faces of the crowd, but no one seemed to notice anything unusual about Charlie. The athletes formed up behind a line at the end of the stadium, and the music stopped. The old man, who Frankie guessed was some sort of referee, raised his rod.

"Come on, Diokles," someone shouted. "Throw like Hercules!"

Diokles must have been the first thrower. He was over six feet tall and built like an ox. He drew back his arm and hurled his discus. It sailed through the air, and thumped down in the sand almost halfway along the arena. The crowd roared and Frankie's heart sank. "That was a massive throw," he whispered to Louise.

She nodded. "I know Charlie can do it, though."

As the next competitor launched

his discus, one of the others coughed loudly, putting him off. The discus wobbled in the air, and landed well short. The spectators groaned.

Frankie frowned. *That doesn't seem fair ...*

"Hey, I can't see," said Max.

Frankie picked up his dog.

They watched as the next athletes prepared to throw. This time a section of the crowd began to boo loudly.

"Not very friendly, are they?" said Louise.

One by one the athletes threw. No one could throw as far as the man called Diokles, especially when the crowd and other competitors were trying to distract them. Last of all, Charlie stepped up empty-handed. He blushed and the referee tutted. "Get this young man a discus. And take off those gloves!"

Frankie held his breath. Charlie *never* took off his gloves.

"I can't," he muttered.

The other athletes all started whispering to each other. Frankie thought he saw something pass between them.

"Then you'll be disqualified," said the referee.

Charlie took off one glove and

laid it on the ground. Diokles handed Charlie a discus. "Good luck, little man," he said with a smirk.

Charlie took the discus.

"Go for it, Charlie!" called Frankie

He rolled his shoulders, took a deep breath, and twisted his hips. The discus flew backwards from his grip, and crashed into the wall of the hut behind.

Everyone burst out laughing.

"Oops," said Max. "Isn't he supposed to throw it the other way?"

Charlie was staring at his hands in dismay.

"Diokles is the winner," cried the referee.

As the huge man lifted his arms in triumph, his hands shone with sweat. Charlie shambled over, head hanging. He showed Frankie his open palm. It was glistening. "There was something greasy on my discus," he said.

Frankie put two and two together. "I think it was Diokles," he said.

Hermes appeared at their side,

sniggering. "Looks like a little oil was spilt."

"They cheated!" said Louise.

Hermes rolled his eyes. "You have to do what you can to win," he said. "Hasn't anyone taught you that? It's the running next. Maybe you'll do better."

A stream of athletes took their places at the start line and Hermes disappeared behind a hut.

"Go on, Frankie," said Charlie. "You're the quickest sprinter on the football team."

"It's one length of the stadium," said Louise. "About a hundred and eighty metres."

Like running from goal to goal on a football pitch, thought Frankie. He jogged to take his place alongside the other athletes. He was still troubled by what had happened with the discus. Weren't the Games supposed to be about fair play?

The whole of the stadium went silent as an official lifted a horn to his lips. Frankie dropped down, hands on the starting line. If he didn't win, it wasn't just his friends he was letting down, but everyone back home whose sports day was ruined.

The runner beside him scowled. "Just stay out of my way, pipsqueak."

The horn sounded and Frankie saw the next runner grab a handful of grit and hurl it right in his face. He blinked madly and threw up his hands as he jolted off the line. By the time he could see again, the other runners were ahead by five metres. *No!*

Frankie powered forward with long strides, trying to catch up. He imagined he was chasing a ball down the wing, trying to overtake a midfielder. He was gaining. The crowd roared. Neck and neck now. Frankie's legs began to burn. He focused on his breaths. *In and out. In and out.* The ground flew

past beneath him. He saw Louise jumping up and down, and Max's tail wagging. He risked a look sideways. *I'm doing it – I'm winning.*

The finishing line was twenty metres away, then ten. Frankie forced his last remaining strength into his pounding thighs . . . .

Ooomph!

The runner on the other side shouldered into him.

Frankie cried out as his legs went from under him, and the ground rose to meet his face.

CHAPTER 5

Frankie slid into the sand and rolled over, a pace short of the finish line. The other runners streaked past, with one bellowing a victory shout.

Dizzy, with grazed arms and legs, Frankie sat up.

"Are you OK?" asked Louise, running over.

Charlie arrived too. "We saw

what happened! The other runner barged you."

Frankie stood shakily, and dusted the sand off his tunic.

The rest of the sprinters were looking at him, breathing heavily.

"He tripped over his own feet," said one.

"Better luck next time," said another.

Frustration burned in Frankie's chest. *I was so close!*

"We should go to the referee," said Louise.

Then he heard a familiar snigger and Hermes appeared from the crowd. "You still don't get it, do you?" he said. "It's every man for himself out here."

"This isn't right," said Frankie. "What happened to 'the best person wins'?"

"You've got to fight dirty to win here," said Hermes. "But look — you've got one more chance. It's long jump next," he said. "Better choose your champion more wisely this time."

More athletes were already lining up at an area marked out in the middle of the arena.

"Are you ready?" Frankie asked Louise.

"Ready for what?" she replied.

"Your turn, of course," said Frankie. "You're the long jump specialist."

Louise's face turned pale. "But it's not the same in the ancient Olympics," she said. "You don't get a run-up. You just jump from standing, using a set of weights in each hand."

"You can do it," said Max. "We believe in you."

Louise smiled. "I'll do my best."

She sprinted off to join the other long jumpers.

"Keep a lookout for anyone cheating," Frankie said to Charlie.

As the competition began,

Frankie saw the strange weights Louise had been talking about. They looked a bit like mini dumb-bells. By swinging them forward and then back they gave the jumper extra distance. The athletes took their turns, throwing their bodies through the air. After each, a marker was placed to show their distance, and the weights were replaced for the next jumper. Finally, it came to Louise's turn.

"Louise is the best in school at long jump," said Charlie. "And there's no oil on those weights."

"I've got my paws crossed for her," said Max.

We need that torch, thought Frankie.

"Oh, no! Something's wrong," said Charlie.

The crowd began to chuckle. Louise was stooping to pick up the jumping weights, but she didn't seem able to lift them at all. Her face was red and straining, but they didn't budge.

"All right, that's enough fooling," said the referee with the rod. "Either take your jump or make way."

Louise tried again with no luck.

"Up there," said Charlie, pointing.

Frankie followed the line of his finger and saw Hermes in one of the tall towers. He was looking at Louise intently and muttering something, waving his snake-wand.

"A spell!" said Frankie. "He's making the weights extra heavy!"

The referee grabbed Louise's shoulder, tugging her back. At the same time her hair came loose from under her hat.

A huge gasp went through the crowd.

"A girl," someone shouted. "Arrest her!"

"Uh-oh," said Charlie, as the spectators began to jostle forwards. "We've been found out."

The shouts of anger rose, and more referees closed in on Louise. Frankie's heart leapt in panic. He pressed towards Louise as well. At this rate, there was going to be a riot! One of the torches on the edge of the arena toppled over as the crowd crashed into it. A shout went up. "Get water!"

"Louise," Frankie cried,

grabbing her arm. "Back to the temple!"

"What about the flame?" she asked.

"Forget it!" said Frankie. "We need to get out of here."

With Charlie on one side, and Frankie on the other, they bustled Louise through the chaos. *We've ruined two sports days!* thought Frankie. They ran back towards the archway that led away from the arena.

"Hey!" called an angry voice. "Stop that dog!"

Frankie looked back and saw Max sprinting full pelt towards him. In his mouth he clutched a flaming torch.

"I've had enough of this!" he said in a muffled voice. "Let's go home!" He scampered up the temple steps.

Frankie saw a mob hot on his heels. He supposed *technically* it was stealing, but Hermes had cheated at every turn. It was the only way.

He ran into the dark temple, between the columns. The black portal home was still there, thank goodness, and Max disappeared through it.

"Don't you want to stay and play a bit more?" said Hermes, flitting above in his winged sandals.

"Not with someone who doesn't play fair!" said Charlie, leaping after Max and vanishing.

Frankie heard footsteps pounding. "Where did they go?" someone cried.

"Time to leave," said Louise, gripping Frankie's hand.

"No, you don't!" cried Hermes, snatching at Frankie. But Louise was already tugging him through the portal ...

Frankie slid across the muddy ground under the goal. For a moment, he felt confused to be back under the grey sky on the school field, but then he saw the football sitting where he'd left it. Max was panting beside Charlie and Louise, with the torch in his jaws. They were all back in their normal clothes.

"Well done, boy!" Frankie said, breathing heavily.

Max whined as the torch sputtered in the falling rain.

"It's going out!" said Charlie.

"Drop, boy," said Frankie, leaning down and taking the torch from his dog's jaws. The flames died into a twist of smoke. "Quick!" said Frankie.

They dashed back across the field, and Frankie held the still-glowing torch to the school's unlit one. He held his breath, willing the flame to ignite. If it didn't, the whole Greek escapade was for nothing.

The torch's glow deepened and flame licked into life.

The effect was instant. Clouds rolled back from the sky, and rays of sun bathed the ground. The rain stopped. Frankie looked down at his wet clothes, then grinned at his friends. The torch from ancient Greece was completely extinguished, but the school flame burned brightly again.

"We did it!" he said.

The doors to the school hall opened, and people began to file into the open air, staring at the clear sky.

"It's global warming, I tell you," said Charlie's dad. "Crazy weather."

Mr Donald led the students out as well. He spied Frankie and his friends and then the blazing torch. He narrowed his eyes. "What are you doing hanging around there?" he asked. "Come on — the sports day is back on!"

Everyone cheered, and Frankie joined the crowd heading back to the sports field. But as the others rushed ahead, Frankie remembered his football and peeled off. It was right where he'd left it, beside the goal. He stooped to pick it up.

Then he noticed something on the ground.

A white feather. Just like the ones on Hermes' sandals.

PART TWO

CHAPTER 6

"It's probably just a bird's feather," said Charlie, when Frankie showed him and Louise what he'd found.

"A pigeon, maybe," added Louise.

The sports day was starting again, so Frankie tried to push his worries out of his mind. Everyone was smiling. Max was back with Frankie's parents and a sulking Kevin on the sidelines. The dry summer ground soaked up all the rain quickly, and soon the only signs of the storm were a few puddles. Mr Donald set out the prize table again at the edge of the pitch, laying the gold, silver and bronze medals beside the makeshift podium. Frankie was glad to be back, but seeing the ancient Olympics in action had left a sour taste in his mouth. Everything they'd learned about sportsmanship had been wrong.

The high jump came first. Frankie's friend Kobe was the tallest in their year by a long way, a defender on their school football team. But a couple of the other schools had tall kids too. It wouldn't be easy.

"Good luck," said Frankie.

Mr Donald set the bar at one metre and fifty centimetres. To Frankie it looked impossibly high, but he knew Kobe would have no problem. His friend started his loping run-up, and sailed over the top. Louise and Charlie clapped, and Kobe's mum and dad beamed proudly. A girl from St Mark's School cleared it too. And the boy from Holly Road. The boy from Mill Lane Lower knocked the bar down, so had to drop out. Mr Donald asked Frankie to help him raise the bar another five centimetres.

This time only Kobe and the girl made it.

"Up to one metre sixty," said Mr Donald.

The tall girl went first and arced over the bar, clearing it by a whisker. She jumped up from the mat on the far side, beaming happily as her friends and family applauded. Kobe looked confident. He bounced towards the bar, and pushed off one foot. Something went wrong, though, and he stumbled, crashing into the bar and sprawling on the mat.

"St Mark's take the gold!" said
Mr Donald. "Better luck next time,
Kobe."

Frankie's friend was shaking his
head. He pointed at his trainers.
"Sir, someone tied my shoelaces
together!"

Mr Donald laughed. "How could

someone tie them together mid-stride?"

Frankie felt uneasy. He scanned the faces of the crowd. No sign of Hermes.

"Relax," said Charlie. "Kobe's laces probably just got tangled."

They made their way over to the sandpit for the long jump. "At least I won't have to use those weights," said Louise, stretching to touch her toes.

Frankie joined her parents to watch the event. Louise's skill was her timing. She managed to get just the right speed and length of stride in her run-up, and soared through

the air. Though the kids from the other schools were good, no one could match her distance. She crashed down into the sand well clear of their markers. Frankie was so happy for his friend to win the gold medal.

"You'll probably make the real Olympics one day," said Charlie, clapping her on the back with a goalie glove as she emerged from the sandpit.

"Thanks," she said, blushing. She winced and scratched at her neck.

"What's wrong?" said Frankie.

Louise started scratching her leg too, then her stomach. Frankie saw the other jumpers clawing at their bodies.

"There must have been something in the sand," said Louise. "I need to wash!" She darted towards the school toilets.

Frankie watched her go with a sinking feeling. "Itching powder ..." he said.

"Are you sure?" said Charlie.

"As sure as I can be," Frankie replied, remembering how Hermes had been holding on to him when he was dragged through the portal. He didn't like this at all. If Hermes *was* here, he could wreck the school sports day.

By the time Louise returned in fresh clothes, Charlie was stepping up for the shot-put. No one seemed to mind that he kept his gloves on here.

There was a huge boy called Hugh from Fallerton Primary, and Frankie saw Charlie eyeing him warily. Hugh looked like he could lift boulders over his head.

"You can do it, Charlie," said Frankie. "Just focus on your technique."

Hugh didn't even need to twist his body. He hurled his shot down the football pitch. It sank into the soggy ground, and he folded his arms smugly. "Beat that," he bellowed.

Several others followed, and no one matched his throw. The closest was a wiry girl from Mill Lane. As Charlie walked up with slumping shoulders, Frankie could see that his friend wasn't hopeful. And in his heart, Frankie knew too that Charlie couldn't beat Hugh's enormous throw.

But that wasn't the point. Normally Charlie would be happy to be taking part.

"Just do your best," he said to Charlie. "That kid's a giant, but you could still get silver."

Charlie took a deep breath and hoisted his arm back. As he released the shot, he cried out as he stumbled and fell. His goalie glove left his hand with the ball attached and landed only a short distance away.

"Hugh wins!" said Mr Donald as the Fallerton boy raised his arms in triumph.

Frankie felt awful for his friend, who looked close to tears. As he walked over to comfort him, Ava, a girl in their class, went to retrieve the glove.

"Hey, Charlie, never mind," said Frankie.

"Mr Donald!" called Eva. Frankie turned to see her frowning, holding the glove and the shot. "I think someone's put glue on the shot."

Mr Donald went over, and inspected the glove. His face darkened. "I think we know who's responsible, don't we?"

Frankie frowned. Did his teacher somehow know about Hermes?

Mr Donald strode away across the pitch.

"Now do you believe that he's here?" Frankie asked his friends.

"I do," said a voice at his ankle.

It was Max, and if Frankie's dog could talk, that meant only one thing. The football's magic was still in the air. But Mr Donald didn't know anything about it, surely. So who did he think was to blame?

Their teacher's voice bellowed across the school field.

"Kevin, come here at once!"

CHAPTER 7

Frankie saw Kevin traipsing across the field.

"It wasn't me, sir," said his brother. "Honest."

"I don't believe you," said Mr Donald. "Shoelaces tied together, itching powder, superglue. It sounds *exactly* like your work, young man."

"But ..."

"Enough," said their teacher. "Why can't you just let others enjoy their day? Wait in the school library until the sports day is finished."

"Not the library, sir!" Kevin exclaimed. But he went inside with the teacher.

"I can't believe I actually feel sorry for your brother," said Charlie.

"So what do we do now?" asked Louise.

"We need to track down Hermes before he ruins everything," said Frankie. "Let's split up."

"And if we find him?" asked Max, growling.

Frankie hadn't really thought that far. He shrugged. "Grab him and don't let go, I suppose."

Louise went off towards the school, Charlie towards the staff car park. Max stuck close to Frankie's ankles as he flitted through the crowd of parents.

"The sooner we find that mischief-maker the better!" said Frankie.

"Follow me," said Max. With his nose to the ground, he veered across the pitch, and towards some trees.

"Are you sure?" said Frankie.

Max kept sniffing. "Yep, he definitely came this way."

He reached the bottom of a tree, and Frankie saw another white feather on the ground. Beside it was a small tube of glue, and an empty packet of itching powder.

"But where's he gone now?" said Frankie.

"There!" said Max, pointing his nose.

Frankie saw movement over by

the winners' podium. Hermes was ducking behind it, looking at the table full of medals. He grabbed a gold medal and looped it around his neck. Then he began to creep away.

Frankie ran towards the podium. "Stop!" He grabbed the ribbon around Hermes' throat.

Hermes jumped, snapping the ribbon as he stumbled out of reach.

Frankie held up the medal. "This does not belong to you! You have to win it fair and square."

"Oh, come on," Hermes said. "We're just having fun. Your world is amazing, by the way. I saw a

chariot made of metal, but without any horse pulling it."

"It's called a car," said Frankie. "And no, we're not having fun," he continued. "You're spoiling everyone's day! Why can't you just play fair?"

"Fair is boring!" said Hermes. He caught sight of something over Frankie's shoulder. "Bye!" With a little jump he was airborne and flying away towards the high branches of a tree.

"Uh-oh," said Max.

Frankie turned and saw what Hermes had spotted. Mr Donald was coming towards him.

"One of the parents told me there was a commotion at the medal table," their teacher said. "What have you got there?"

Frankie blushed. *This is getting worse by the second.* He held out the medal.

Mr Donald looked shocked. "I expected better of you, Frankie," he said. "You have to win a medal fair and square. What made you take it?"

Frankie could hardly explain that his magic football had taken him to ancient Greece and he'd accidentally brought a mischievous god home with him. But if he

admitted to stealing, he'd probably
be sent to spend the rest of the
sports day with Kevin.

*And then there'll be no stopping
Hermes . . .*

Frankie nodded to Max. "It was
my dog, sir. He grabbed a medal
and I ran after him to get it back."

Max looked up and whined.

Sorry, boy, thought Frankie.

Mr Donald sighed. "Did he? Well,
perhaps you should keep him on a
lead from now on."

"I will, sir," said Frankie.

Mr Donald held out his hand and
Frankie dropped the medal into
his palm. "Time for your football

event," said his teacher. "With your brother out of the way, at least there'll be no more mischief."

He turned and headed back towards the pitch. With a heavy heart, Frankie followed his teacher.

CHAPTER 8

Mr Donald and several helpers were laying out the obstacle course, and placing footballs on the pitch. The game was straightforward — a race to the halfway line, get a ball and dribble it around several cones, then flick it up and head it through a hoop. Last of all, at the edge of the penalty box, a shot at goal. The parents lined both sides of the pitch, with the main crowd at the far end, near the finishing goal.

Frankie made sure his boots were laced tightly and jumped up and down to get his legs warm. He looked down the line at the other competitors. He recognized most of them, football players from the other schools who he'd played against several times. Two down was Nate Adams, from Mill Lane. Frankie knew how good he was — fast and skillful. He would be the main threat.

Mr Donald stood to one side, his whistle hanging around his neck. He lifted it to his lips, and Frankie lowered himself into a half-crouch.

As the whistle went, he burst forwards for his second race of the day. Nate pulled ahead a fraction. Frankie saw another boy at the far side keeping pace and a girl to his left as well. It was the Fallerton keeper – he hadn't realised she was so quick. He pumped his arms and reached the halfway line in joint second place.

Picking up the ball, he tried to stay calm. The key to the cones was taking it steady and not making a mistake. The girl faltered and knocked over a cone – automatic disqualification. Nate was level with Frankie. The other boy glided smoothly around the obstacles.

Frankie didn't have time to look at him properly — he kept his eyes on the cones.

He came out at the end a fraction behind Nate.

The hoops were all suspended from a cord across the pitch. Nate overbalanced on his header, and it flew wide. *Ha!* Frankie stopped the ball under his foot, rocked it back on to his toe and flicked it up. Just a small bump with his head sent it through the hoop. He'd done it! Now just the shot, and the gold was his!

He lined up the ball with a single touch and blasted it towards the middle of the goal.

A sudden gust of wind caught the ball and sent it spinning over the crossbar. Frankie staggered to a halt.

Then another ball buried into the back of the net.

"Supergoal!" yelled a voice.

Frankie turned to see a boy wearing a PE kit and a crafty smile. *Hermes!*

"You!" he said.

One by one, the other competitors arrived and shot at the target. Soon there were six or more balls in the back of the net.

"This game's easier than it looks!" said Hermes. There was no sign of his winged sandals now – he

was wearing football boots. Frankie
wondered where he'd got the kit
from. Probably the lost property
basket. Or he'd just used magic.
*What does it matter now? I'm out
and he's won.*

Mr Donald blew his whistle
again. "We have a winner!"

The crowd applauded quietly.

Frankie guessed they all thought Hermes must be from one of the other schools.

"Don't look like such a sore loser," said Mr Donald. "It's only a game, Frankie. That's the end of the sports day. There'll be a break for refreshments before the medal ceremony. Juice, tea and coffee outside the school hall."

The spectators and kids began to file off the sports pitch. Frankie's own parents stopped by him. "Never mind," said Frankie's dad. "You were doing really well until the end. It looked like a freak wind."

Frankie could hardly look him

in the eye. *A freak wind? Magic mischief, more like!* And what was worse, Hermes would get a gold medal he didn't deserve. The magic football had ruined everything! Frankie felt like getting it and throwing it in the bin.

"Hey, Frankie," Louise said softly. "We all know you're the real winner."

Charlie put a comforting glove on his shoulder. "Lou's right, you know."

Frankie's fury drained away. There were more important things than medals.

Max growled, and they all span around to see Hermes.

"Had your fun now?" said Louise.

Hermes smiled. "Oh, I'm just getting started!"

"What do you mean?" said Charlie.

Hermes pointed towards the school hall. "I looked in your temple there. Quite a display. The Olympics are still going! And not just in Greece, either. All over the world."

Frankie didn't like the glint in Hermes' eyes. "It's nothing like in your time," he said. "People pride themselves on being honest, competing by the rules."

Hermes stuck his fingers in his ears. "Oh, please! I think I might pay the real Olympic Games a visit, actually. Shake things up a bit."

Frankie felt the blood drain from his face. "You . . . you can't!"

He tried to grab the boy, but Hermes slipped away among the other students and parents.

"Do you think he's serious?" asked Charlie.

Frankie didn't know. He couldn't even imagine the sort of havoc Hermes might wreak at the real Olympic Games in front of billions of people.

There's no way I'll let that happen.

"We need to get him back where he belongs," said Frankie.

Charlie nodded. "We could wait for the ceremony. Something tells me he's not going to leave without his medal."

Frankie chewed his lip. If they tried to capture Hermes outside the school building, he'd just fly away. Plus, everyone would see and there'd be a *lot* of explaining to do. They needed to lure him indoors. And for that, they needed bait. "I have a better idea," he said.

"What?" asked Louise.

"We're going to show Hermes that we can play a trick too," he said. "And we need Kevin."

CHAPTER 9

Frankie led the others to the school library. They found Kevin shelving books. It was one of Mr Donald's favourite punishments.

"Come to gloat?" sneered Kevin.

"Actually, we need your help," said Frankie.

"Oh?" said his brother.

"It's a long story," said Frankie, "but the football—"

"I *knew* there was something weird going on," interrupted Kevin.

"Just listen, will you?" said Louise.

Frankie explained as quickly as he could what had happened with Hermes.

"You've really messed up this

time," said Kevin with a wicked smile. "You're in *so* much trouble."

"The whole future of the Olympics is being threatened here," said Louise. "He'll wreck every event."

"I don't see why I should help you," grumbled Frankie's brother.

"It was all your fault!" said Charlie. "If you hadn't put out the flame—"

Frankie nudged their friend. He needed his brother on their side, and he thought he knew a way to convince him.

"Fine, Kev," he said. "I guess it is a bit dangerous. If you're scared . . ."

"Hey, I'm not scared," said Kev.

"Maybe I didn't mean *scared*," said Frankie. "Hermes is really clever, though. And daring. You should see some of naughty things he does ..."

"He sounds pretty childish if you ask me," said Kevin. "Itching powder – come on!"

"Yeah, but he let *you* take the blame," said Louise. She obviously realised what Frankie was trying to do.

Kevin glowered. "Yeah, he did."

"And here you are stacking library books," said Frankie, "while Hermes is getting a gold medal."

Kevin clenched his fists. "Right, how do we get him?"

Frankie smiled. *Now comes the tricky part.*

Five minutes later, after Frankie had shared his plan, everyone was heading back out to the medal ceremony. As Charlie had guessed, Hermes was loitering among them. *No doubt looking forward to picking up his gold medal.*

"What school did you say you were at, Herbert?" asked Mr Donald.

"I didn't," replied Hermes. He slipped away from Frankie's teacher.

"Go on," said Frankie, giving Kevin a light shove. "Time to act your part."

They hung back a little as Kevin fell in beside Hermes. Frankie listened closely.

"Hey," said Kevin. "Do you know who I am?"

"You're that Frankie boy's brother," Hermes replied.

"That's right," said Kevin. "And guess what — I like mischief almost as much as you."

"I doubt that," said Hermes.

"Problem is," said Kevin, "my brother's always snitching on me."

Frankie swallowed. Would Hermes fall for it?

"He's a bit of a goody–two–shoes, isn't he?" said the boy god.

"Well, I've got an idea to cause some mischief," said Kevin. "If you're up for it?"

Hermes stopped and a smile curled his lips. "Tell me."

Two minutes later, in the school changing room. Frankie and Louise crouched under layers of clothes. Charlie was hiding behind the door.

"Do you think he'll fall for it?" whispered Louise.

"Hermes only cares about making

trouble," said Frankie. "Ready, Max?" he asked.

"Ready," came Max's muffled voice.

"They're coming!" hissed Charlie.

Sure enough, Frankie heard footsteps, then voices.

"... so this football can take me anywhere?" Hermes was saying. "I could go to the real Olympics?"

"Anywhere in the world — and into the past, too," said Kevin. "All in the blink of an eye. My brother keeps it to himself because he doesn't want anyone else to have fun."

Frankie peered through the hanging coats and saw the two

of them approach the door of the changing room. Hermes was rubbing his hands together in glee.

"We need to find his sports bag," said Frankie's brother, peering around the changing room. He pointed to a holdall marked with the badge of Liverpool FC.

Frankie's mouth was dry as he watched Hermes approach. They almost had him . . .

Hermes grabbed the zip and tugged it back.

Max poked his furry head out. "Surprise!"

Hermes staggered back, knocking into Kevin.

"What's going on?" he cried.

Charlie slammed the door closed. "A trap!" he said. "And you fell for it – hook, line and sinker."

Frankie and Louise burst out from behind the coats. Frankie went to a bag with a Chelsea logo – his real bag – and took out the magic football.

"I'd *never* support Liverpool," he said. "That's Louise's bag."

Hermes looked at Kevin. "You tricked me!"

Kevin grinned. "Call yourself the god of mischief! Pathetic."

"Time to give up," said Frankie,

holding up the football. "We're sending you home."

Hermes glared at each of them in turn. "You'll have to catch me first."

He jumped into the air, and his boots transformed into winged sandals.

"Get him!" cried Frankie, leaping up. Hermes flew out of reach, and Max began to bark, chasing him around the room. Charlie and Louise and Kevin all joined in the pursuit, hopping on to benches and snatching at the air. Hermes wheeled about, plucking at coats and bags and dropping them down.

Soon the room was in chaos. They tripped over the fallen debris and each other in an effort to seize the flying boy. Frankie managed to grab an ankle and hauled Hermes down into a pile of coats. He felt the boy flailing and lost his grip as the others piled in too.

"I've got an arm!" said Charlie.

"That's *my* arm!" said Kevin.

Frankie pushed a smelly shirt off his head, and untangled himself from Louise. He was holding a winged sandal, but no Hermes.

Max emerged from the pile with the other sandal in his jaws.

"Where'd he go?" he growled.

"That way!" said Kevin.

Frankie groaned. The changing room door was swinging open. Hermes had escaped again!

CHAPTER 10

"Catch him!" said Louise. Max scampered through the door after Hermes, but Frankie began pulling off his shoes.

"What are you doing?" said Charlie. "This is no time to get changed!"

Frankie wasn't sure it would work, but he guessed Hermes still had magical god powers. They needed an advantage. He tugged on the winged sandals. *Perhaps I can even up the odds,* he thought.

As soon as the sandals were on his feet, Frankie felt different. Lighter, more nimble. "No wonder he was so good in the football race," he muttered.

"Do you think you can make them work?" said Louise.

"Let's try," said Frankie. He willed the shoes to flap.

But nothing happened.

"We're wasting time," said Kevin, rushing through the door as well.

But Frankie could sense the

magic lurking. He closed his eyes.
Come on – fly!

His stomach flipped and he heard
Louise cry, "Woah!"

Then his head banged into
something and he opened his
eyes. He was hovering near the
ceiling. Luckily the tiles were only
polystyrene, or he'd have knocked
himself out.

"You're flying!" said Charlie.

Frankie looked at his flapping feet in astonishment. He angled his body towards the door and shot forward, crashing into the doorframe and bouncing off.

"Ouch!" he said. "This is harder than it looks."

He edged through the door slowly, trying to keep himself steady.

"Well, you'd better learn quick," said Louise. "Come on!"

She ran down the corridor outside. Frankie could hear Max barking wildly somewhere nearby. He shot along the passage, above

Louise and Charlie's heads. He whizzed round a corner, narrowly avoiding a light on the wall. At the far end of the corridor outside the head's office was Kevin, sitting on the ground and rubbing his head. Max was scrabbling to free himself from a bin.

"He went that way!" said Kevin, pointing towards the hall.

Frankie used his feet to guide himself at breakneck speed past his brother. Barely in control, it felt amazing and scary at the same time. He flew into the hall to see Hermes standing on the stage. The boy god threw out a hand, and a blast of wind punched Frankie in the chest. It flipped him round in the air. He crashed into the display of Olympic rings, sending them scattering to the ground, but managed to steady himself.

"Those are my sandals!" said Hermes.

"You can have them back if you agree to go home," said Frankie. Through the windows, he could see the medal ceremony beginning on the sports field. If anyone looked back this way, they'd get a nasty shock.

"I don't take orders from mortals," snapped Hermes. "I'm a god!"

Louise, Charlie and Kevin all burst into the hall too. Max followed shortly after.

"You're surrounded!" said Frankie.

Hermes shots blasts of wind at them all, whipping their clothes and hair. One blast knocked Louise off her feet. Charlie and Kevin both fought against the gales. Pictures tore from the walls, and Max skidded back across the polished floor. Frankie swooped down and snatched up one of the rings.

Hermes shot gust after gust at Frankie, but he dodged and weaved on his winged feet like a fighter pilot. He was getting nearer all the time. When he was close enough, he hurled the ring and it looped over Hermes' head, trapping his arms against his side. Charlie, Louise and Kevin darted in too, tossing the other plastic hoops over his head. Last of all Max ran up with a ring in his jaws. With a jerk of his head, he hooked it under Hermes' feet. The boy god tripped and landed with a thump on his side.

The winds died away, and Hermes lay back with a moan.

"All right," he sighed. "You win. Fair and square."

*

The hall was a mess, but nothing was broken.

While the others watched Hermes, Frankie aimed the magic football at the map of ancient Greece on the wall. It was just about the only bit of the display that had survived. When the ball hit, the picture vanished, revealing the dim interior of the Temple of Zeus.

"My dad's going to be really angry this time," said Hermes. For once, he looked serious.

"Who's your dad?" asked Frankie.

"Him," said Hermes, pointing to the statue of Zeus. "He banned me from taking part in the Olympics after I won the running race. He said I cheated."

"Did you?" asked Louise.

Hermes blushed. "Maybe a bit. I just wanted to make him proud."

Frankie felt a twinge of sympathy. "You'll make him proud by just doing your best," he said.

Hermes's face brightened. "You think so?"

"Yes!" said everyone.

The boy god smiled. "I'll give it a try," he said. "Can I at least have my shoes back?"

Frankie looked down at the winged sandals on his feet. He'd

have loved to keep them, but despite Hermes' trouble-making, they belonged to him. He pulled them off and threw them into the portal.

"There you go."

Hermes smiled. "We had fun, didn't we?"

"No!" everyone answered.

Hermes shrugged. "All right, all right. I get the message."

Frankie couldn't help smiling. *I suppose he really can't help it. He* is *the god of mischief after all.*

"Goodbye," he said.

Hermes gave a little wave and jumped through the portal. As soon as he vanished, the map reappeared. Frankie picked up his football. "We'd better clear up."

They set about sticking the pictures back on the walls. The rings would have to wait for the caretaker and his ladder.

They'd just finished when Mr Donald appeared at the doors.

"What are you doing in here?" he said. "We're giving out the medals. I thought I said to put that dog on a lead!"

They all ran outside, and Frankie and Charlie stood beside Louise's parents as she climbed to the top podium to receive her gold for the long jump.

"I won't forget this sports day for a long time," said Charlie as he clapped, "even though I came last in the shot-put."

There was a bit of confusion when it came to the medals for the football. Mr Donald didn't seem to know who had won the gold. No one did. The top spot of the podium remained empty.

"Where is that boy?" called Frankie's teacher. "What was his name? Herman?"

Frankie smiled. He wondered if Hermes had really learned his lesson, or if he would go back to his cheating ways. What mattered, though, was that the Olympic spirit was alive and well. Hermes hadn't had chance to ruin the Games.

Frankie found he didn't mind Nate getting the silver. He clapped louder than anyone. In fact, he didn't care about medals at all any more.

Charlie's right – it was an adventure to remember.

And sometimes just playing fair was enough.

ACKNOWLEDGEMENTS

Many thanks to everyone at Hachette Children's Group; Neil Blair, Zoe King, Daniel Teweles and all at The Blair Partnership; Luella Wright for bringing my characters to life; special thanks to Michael Ford for all his wisdom and patience; and to Steve Kutner for being a great friend and for all his help and guidance, not just with the book but with everything.

**Turn the page for
an exclusive extract from
Frankie's next adventure,
The Elf Express,
coming soon!**

Frankie's family, Louise and Charlie are spending Christmas in Austria with Frankie's pen pal, Heidi, who has taken them out to the slopes to learn how to ski.

They all climbed on to the ski lift. Most of the other people were heading off the slopes, Frankie noticed. It was Christmas Eve, after all, and they were probably going to get warm and cosy by their fires. Frankie's parents had been decorating the Christmas tree at their chalet with Heidi's mum and dad. Frankie's family and closest friends were staying with his pen pal over the holiday. It was great to spend time with them all — and such a great chance to learn how to ski!

As they rose up the mountain, Frankie saw the distant cloud more clearly. It was moving fast on high winds. He shivered. The mountains were incredible, but Heidi's brother loved telling stories about all the things that could go wrong — white-outs, avalanches and frostbite.

By the time they reached the top of the green run again, Frankie's

fingers and toes were cold, and
the sun was hidden by cloud. "Let's
make this quick," he said.

"I'm doing the black run," said
Kevin. He stayed on the lift as it
climbed higher.

"That's silly, Kev," called Frankie.
So far they'd just been on the green
piste — the easiest. Black runs were
for experienced skiers.

"I'd better go with him," said
Heidi, clambering back on to the
lift. "See you all at the bottom?"

Frankie nodded. They were lucky
they had Heidi with them — she'd
been skiing since before she could
even walk.

He, Louise and Charlie lined up at the top of the green slope. "I'm looking forward to a hot chocolate," said Charlie, flexing his goalie gloves on the tops of his ski poles.

"Didn't you fancy wearing proper ski gloves?" asked Louise.

Charlie looked at her as if she was mad, and Louise grinned. They all knew Charlie never took off his goalie gloves, even though a game of football looked very unlikely three thousand metres up an icy mountain.

"Let's go!" said Frankie, edging off.

This time he reached the bottom

without falling over once. Louise and Charlie clapped their hands.

"I wonder how Heidi and Kevin are doing?" said Frankie, peering further up the mountain.

"We can't just stand around," said Louise, stepping off her snowboard. "It's too cold. Let's head to the bottom of the black run to meet them."

They clipped off their hire skis, and handed them in at the café. Frankie shouldered his rucksack. They walked through the snow and arrived at the black run just in time to see Kevin sliding down on his back, skis at an angle. He bumped into the barrier with a groan. Heidi swished to a halt beside him.

"What happened?" asked Frankie. "Are you OK?"

Kevin grimaced through a face-full of snow. "Twisted my ankle," he said, blushing.

"What a surprise," grumbled Charlie.

"You could have been badly hurt!" said Heidi. She looked more annoyed than Frankie had ever seen her. He felt embarrassed. *Why can't Kevin just behave himself?*

The sky darkened suddenly as the cloud swept overhead. Snow

swirled around them, thick and fast, and the ski lifts clanked. Heidi looked worried.

"We don't have time to return to the chalet," she said. "My grandfather has a cabin a little way down the mountain. We can shelter there until the storm is over."

"Mum and Dad will be worried," said Frankie.

"It's OK, there's a phone," said Heidi. "Storms here can be very bad so we must stay safe."

Supporting Kevin between them, they trudged down the mountainside. The snow continued to fall heavily and a wind gusted through the trees. Frankie felt a little bit afraid.

"Not much further now," said Heidi.

It was already hard to see more than twenty or thirty metres ahead, and off the main slope the snow was so thick that Frankie kept sinking over his ankles. He heard a rumble of thunder from the sky. Or was it an avalanche? He peered at the mountaintops, but they were hidden by clouds.

I hope Heidi can get us out of this . . .

Competition Time

COULD YOU BE A WINNER LIKE FRANKIE?

Every month one lucky fan will win an exclusive
Frankie's Magic Football goodie bag! Here's how to enter:

Every **Frankie's Magic Football** book
features different animals. Go to:
www.frankiesmagicfootball.co.uk/competitions
and name three different animals that feature in three
different **Frankie's Magic Football** books.
Then you could be a winner!

You can also send your entry by post by filling in
the form on the opposite page.

Once complete, please send your entries to:

Frankie's Magic Football Competition
Hachette Children's Books, Carmelite House,
50 Victoria Embankment,
London, EC4Y 0DZ

GOOD LUCK!

Competition Entry Page

Please enter your details below:

1. Name of Frankie Book: ....
   Animal: ....

2. Name of Frankie Book: ....
   Animal: ....

3. Name of Frankie Book: ....
   Animal: ....

My name is: ....

My date of birth is: ....

Email address: ....

Address 1: ....

Address 2: ....

Address 3: ....

County: ....

Post Code: ....

Parent/Guardian signature: ....

FRANKIE'S MAGIC FOOTBALL
WEBSITE

Have you had a chance to check out
frankiesmagicfootball.co.uk yet?

Get involved in **competitions**, find out **news** and
updates about the series, play **games** and watch
videos featuring the author, **Frank Lampard!**

Visit the site to join
Frankie's FC today!